The Picture of Nobody

RABINDRANATH MAHARAJ

The Picture of Nobody

Grass Roots Press

First published in 2010 by Grass Roots Press

The Good Reads series is funded in part by the Government of Canada's Office of Literacy and Essential Skills.

Grass Roots Press also gratefully acknowledges the financial support for its publishing programs provided by the following agencies: the Government of Canada through the Canada Book Fund and the Government of Alberta through the Alberta Foundation for the Arts.

Alberta
Foundation
for the Arts

Grass Roots Press would also like to thank ABC Life Literacy Canada for their support. Good Reads® is used under licence from ABC Life Literacy Canada.

Library and Archives Canada Cataloguing in Publication

Maharaj, Rabindranath, 1955–
    The picture of nobody / Rabindranath Maharaj.

(Good reads series)
ISBN 978–1–926583–28–0

    1. Readers for new literates. I. Title. II. Series: Good reads series (Edmonton, Alta.)

PS8576.A42P53 2010   428.6'2   C2010–902137–1

Printed and bound in Canada.

Distributed to libraries and educational and community organizations by
Grass Roots Press
www.grassrootsbooks.net

Distributed to retail outlets by
HarperCollins Canada Ltd.
www.harpercollins.ca

Chapter One

Just two weeks after my family moved to Ajax, I saw my parents glued to the television. At first, I thought they were watching a movie. People were rushing out from a tunnel. A man in a heavy coat led out a lady wearing what looked like a gas mask. It was caked with thick white dust. I wondered what the lady's face looked like behind the mask. Was she crying, or were her eyes closed in fright? Then the scene shifted to a red double-decker bus. It seemed to have been smashed with a giant hammer.

"There is nothing sadder than smoke," my father said. "It always marks the end of something." Dad usually spoke like this. Quoting the dead poet Shakespeare, or saying things only he could understand.

Mom placed a finger against her lips to silence Dad. On the television, a woman was sitting on the pavement. Why wasn't the woman running with everyone else? Then the camera focused on a small body beside her. I waited for a commercial to come on. Then I asked, "What's going on? Where's this happening?"

"In far-away London," Mom said in a sad voice. "Terrorists have bombed three subway trains and that bus." After a while, she added, "What's happening is madness."

"Can something like that happen here?" Allison, my sister, asked.

My mother looked through the balcony door. I wondered if she was considering all the places she had lived. First of all, Uganda, in Africa, where she had grown up and then met and married Dad. Then Australia. She and Dad had moved there after the cruel ruler of Uganda and his army had destroyed the homes and businesses of all their friends. Then Fredericton, a town in New Brunswick, close to the east coast of Canada. Both Allison and I were born there.

Then, after seven years, Napanee, in Ontario, where Dad got a job at a mill. And finally here, Ajax, a bit east of Toronto. "Who knows, dear," she said softly, as if speaking to herself. "But not in Ajax."

During the following weeks, I got a good idea why my parents felt so comfortable in Ajax. Everything seemed squeezed together. We could walk to the library, the hospital, the schools, the lake, and the shopping malls. Everyone seemed to know each other, and the parks were usually crowded with old people walking about or chatting on benches.

One day, we were driving through narrow streets with old wartime houses on either side. Mom pointed to the signs and said the streets were all named after the sailors from some old battleship. "No one is ashamed of their past here," she said.

Mom felt that Canada was the most perfect place in the world. All the bad things happened elsewhere. She pointed this out to Dad whenever he began talking of his boyhood in Uganda. Dad would answer that "his people" were nomads. His great-grandfather had moved from India to

Uganda, he and Mom had moved to Australia, and now they had moved to Canada. His favourite saying — when he was not quoting Shakespeare — was, "Everything is temporary."

I really hoped that Dad was wrong and that our stay in Ajax would be permanent. I was sad when we moved from Fredericton and I had to leave all of my friends behind. Because of that, I made few friends in Napanee. I did not want to be disappointed again.

Ajax was different. We did not live in a small house, as we had in the other places, but on the tenth floor of a high-rise. From the balcony, I could see the playground and the hospital. I believed that if we stayed in Ajax, I would finally make some friends. I had to. Everyone was squashed together. Sometimes I pretended that everyone in our high-rise — the men, women, and children I spotted on the elevator or in the parking lot — belonged to one big family. After all, we lived in the same building.

Yet, only five months after we moved to Ajax, Allison told me something terrible. Our parents, she said, were thinking of moving once more. She hoped they would pick Toronto.

Chapter Two

I couldn't believe what Allison had said. Surely Mom and Dad weren't thinking of moving. Didn't Mom say that small towns like Ajax were safe?

That Friday evening, at the dinner table, my mother asked her usual question, "Do you like your new school?" I guess she wanted to know if I had made any new friends.

Before I could answer, my father began one of his long speeches. As usual, it was about his childhood in Uganda. I knew what would come next. In the beginning, they were so poor that they didn't waste a single scrap of anything. He and his three brothers worked every day in their father's clothing store, Baba's Emporium (such a grand word for "shop"!). They kept working there, even when they grew up to be young men. When they were chased out of the country by the government, Dad's father had said, "This is just a new opportunity." And the family split up to find these new opportunities. Dad's parents went to England and his brothers went to Singapore, Australia, and Canada.

I had heard this hard-luck story a hundred times, but that night I had an insight. If I had been in a cartoon, a light bulb would have appeared up above my head. This is what I suddenly knew: Dad's nomad story was just a cover. He moved so much because he was scared of being chased away once more. He would rather choose to move than be forced to move. No longer would others control his decisions.

I ate in silence as my father continued his story. At the end of the meal, I had another light-bulb moment. I had to convince my father that Ajax was different. He would never be chased from this town, where people seemed to spend their entire lives.

Allison, who was eighteen months younger than me, believed there was a pattern to all our moves. Each move brought us closer to Toronto. That city would surely come next. She seemed thrilled by the idea of moving there.

One night, both of us were watching the news on the living room TV. Allison said, "Everything's happening in Toronto." As she continued, I saw that, for her, Toronto was some sort of magical place, with concerts and formal dances and costume parties and festivals. Only young and beautiful people lived in her sparkling city. Maybe she believed that they shipped all the old folks to places like Ajax.

"The festivals would be so much fun," she said.

"There are also festivals here," I told her.

She slumped on the couch and said, "Yeah, but just for old people. Jam and pickle festivals."

"What about the lake? There are always games and other activities going on there."

"Some people have grown up. In case you haven't noticed," she said.

I realized that Allison would be no help in convincing my parents that Ajax was a great little town. In fact, soon I was sure she was sabotaging me. Every time I pointed out something good, she shot it down. One day, when we were bringing the groceries in from the car, I said, "The hospital is so close you can see it from the parking lot."

"Yeah. And you can hear the ambulances all night."

Another morning, Mom was packing our school lunches. I said, "You should take a break, Mom. We can get really good food in the school cafeteria."

Allison added, "And have you noticed that all the black and white and brown kids sit in their own separate spots?"

No, I had not noticed that, but I would not give up. "I'm sure it's the same in Toronto."

I tried to think of good things about Ajax that Allison could not sabotage. That evening, when my parents were watching the news, I said in a fake-casual voice, "There's hardly any crime here. All the gangs seem to live in Toronto."

"There's nothing here to steal," Allison said. "Except for flower pots and garden gnomes." I had to admire Allison: she had not missed a beat. I realized at that moment that I would have to come up with a smarter plan. I would have to find something special about Ajax that Allison could not strike down.

I focused on the old wartime houses that looked like gingerbread cottages and the tidy playgrounds filled with mothers and chubby babies. I began sitting at different tables in the school cafeteria. I listened to conversations, hoping someone would reveal a secret about Ajax. A secret so special that my father would never want to leave. But the other students just got quiet. Sometimes they glanced at each other and then back at me. I wished I could make friends as easily as Allison.

After school, I usually walked to the library to work on my grade twelve science projects. The library was just a ten-minute walk from my school. I usually stayed for an hour or so, until the bells in the tower of the nearby town hall told me the time was five o'clock. I would not have been surprised if someday the clock forgot the hour. Ajax would be like some sleepy little town in a *Twilight Zone* episode. Time would stand still.

Sometimes I tried to eavesdrop in the library, especially when I noticed a quiet conversation.

Once, I missed the five o'clock bells. When I got home, my mother asked where I had been.

"There's free internet at the library," I told her. "And Allison is always using our computer." I didn't mention that the family computer in the living room was too close to the television. The last thing I wanted was Mom thinking that the apartment was too small.

"She's chatting on the computer with her old friends from Napanee," my mother said. Her voice sounded flat.

I'd always felt that Mom chose that tone to start my father talking about the past. And just as I expected, Dad chimed in about kids nowadays forever hiding away inside their little private worlds. Back in Uganda, a family was like a little community. Everything was shared. Even secrets. "*The secrets of our hearts*," Dad recited in his Shakespeare voice. Allison said that Facebook was the same as Dad's Uganda, except she could share secrets with way more people. Facebook was an even bigger family.

Maybe I was desperate, but right then I had another light-bulb moment. Dad was always talking about how he and his brothers cooperated in Uganda. What if I showed him that Allison and I could get along just as well? Wouldn't he think that Ajax had something to do with it? I could not bring back Dad's young life in Uganda, but I would remind him of what he missed most of all.

Chapter Three

Now, I should say straight off that Allison and I had never been close. We looked different, too. I was dark and chubby, like Dad, while Allison got Mom's big eyes and light brown colour. But Mom seemed satisfied with everything around her. Allison behaved like a bratty kid.

I couldn't help thinking that our parents treated her better than they treated me, too. She got birthday and Christmas presents of fancy dresses and pink shoes and spiteful-looking dolls. All I got were science books, telescopes, and chemistry sets.

It seemed they always took her side during our arguments. They never praised me for my high marks in school nor criticized my sister's average marks. Dad would say that, as the older child, I was supposed to set a proper example. And Mom would stand next to Allison as if they were on the same football team.

Allison had learned to roll her eyes and rock her head in one smooth motion. I know it might seem a simple act. But with it, she could blame me, laugh at me, and brag about herself, all at the same time. Worse, she did it so swiftly that neither of my parents ever noticed. Once I tried to imitate her, and she burst into laughter. It was so unfair!

I started to feel that the world really favoured women. When I told my mother what I thought, she cried, "Have you gone crazy?"

In some countries, she told me, it was bad luck to make a baby girl. Girls couldn't go to school, drive cars, stay out late, or even choose their own husbands. Mom was so upset that day that I never brought up the topic again.

Later, recalling Mom's list of women's troubles, I got an idea. The following day after school, I spotted Allison walking all by herself. I hurried to catch up with her. When I did, she seemed annoyed and walked even faster.

"Hey, do you know there's a girls' soccer team in Ajax?"

"So?"

"Maybe you could join."

"I hate soccer."

"There's also a girls' basketball team. And badminton, too."

She kept silent, but as soon as we got home, she went to my mother in the kitchen. "I think Tommy should get a hobby," Allison said. "He's been staring at all these athletic girls."

For once, my mother took my side. "Well, he's a big boy now. Even though he still has his chubby baby cheeks. It's time he found himself a nice girl."

Allison did one of her eye-rolling things. Except this time, she added a couple of snorty chuckles. Mom glanced at my face, and she began to laugh, which made me think that she had not taken my side after all.

Still, I was determined to find some way to prove to my parents that Allison and I were getting along, no matter how hard that might be. I wished I understood her better. Especially why she seemed so annoyed when I spoke to her at school. One recess, I noticed her with a tall girl who wore black clothes. They matched her dark lipstick and eyeliner. The girl looked quite fierce. I was about to tell my sister that her new friend looked like trouble. But instead I said, "Your friend seems interesting. What's her name?"

"Aranka."

"What sort of name is that?"

"Hungarian. And she's not interested in you." Her glance suggested that I should stick with looking at the girls' soccer team. Still, I didn't mind, because now I knew something more about her.

Soon I saw Allison hanging out with more girls who were dressed like her new friend. She began wearing dark eyeliner, too. One morning, she appeared in the kitchen wearing a wide studded belt. Two thick chains ran from the belt into the pockets of her pants.

"What's this?" Dad asked her.

I saw my opportunity. "It's a look. A lot of the girls at school dress like this."

Mom said to Allison, "It's better than being a Valley Girl, anyway. Everything 'so, like, oh my God'? All that 'totally' and 'whatever'?" She smiled at the memory.

But Dad was not as impressed. "It makes her look like a vampire, if you ask me."

"I think she's imitating Xena the Warrior Princess, on TV."

The minute I looked at Allison, I knew she did not appreciate my help. She put on a long, trailing winter coat. On our way to school, she told me, "It's Goth, okay? And it's a better style than you and your geeky friends have."

What friends? I thought. But she had hurried away.

I realized that having a friendship with my sister would be impossible. I was not in her league.

Chapter Four

After I gave up on Allison, I got a clue to why she believed our parents would soon leave Ajax. During dinner, Dad told Mom that an American company had quit ordering computer chips. I guess that's what they made at the factory where he worked. Just to annoy Mom, he said he might soon have to get a job driving a taxicab. He had said the same thing when we were leaving Napanee and Fredericton. And just like those times, Mom reminded him that he was too educated for that sort of job.

"Is it for this reason you came to Canada, Aggy?"

Aggy is Mom's nickname for Dad. I think it's because we're Ismaili Muslims, and our leader is the Aga Khan. Dad talks about him all the time, even though, as far as I know, we're not religious.

Dad liked to be asked about why they left Uganda. Talking about those days prompted him to recall his own dream of becoming a professor. In this dream, instead of sorting and packing things in a factory, he sat in an office that was stuffed with books. Sometimes Dad would tell me that he would have reached this goal if he had stayed in Uganda. Mom would never miss the chance to add, "Or if you had been born in Canada."

All my life, I had felt that both of my parents were pushing a burden onto my back. As if I was supposed to fulfil my father's dream in some way. It was really unfair. Why me?

Why me? Well, as I grew older, I slowly began to understand this burden. I also got a better grasp of Dad's Uganda stories. He and his brothers had worked in their father's store every evening after school. For sure, working instead of studying had blocked his ambition. That was why he had never asked me to get an after-school job, even though I was seventeen years old. He was determined that nothing would stand between me and my education.

Maybe that had been a good plan, but now Dad's factory was possibly going to lay him off. He needed my help.

Each day, on my way home from the library, I studied the strip mall. There was a bus terminal, with a long line of GO buses going west to Toronto and east to Oshawa. Behind the buses were a dollar store, a bakery, a drugstore, and a video store. I was sure none of these stores would hire me, because I had no work experience. However, there was also a sort of run-down coffee shop named Sip and Sup. Two picnic tables sat outside. Maybe the owner wanted to create a sidewalk café. But the young men who sat there just smoked and gazed at the schoolgirls crossing the parking lot.

One day, I walked into Sip and Sup. There were a couple of old people sipping and supping. They were also slurping. I couldn't stand that sound. Maybe the owner should have named it Sip and Slurp.

I was about to walk out when a small Chinese man behind the counter yelled at me: "What you want? Yes?"

Was he used to shouting at the old people, who couldn't hear properly? He surprised me so much that I blurted out, "I'm looking for a job."

"Busy today. Come back tomorrow and I tell you. Hah!" He laughed in one sharp explosion.

I looked at all the empty tables, and on my way home I was sure he had meant: *Bugger off. Come back tomorrow and I kill you. Nya ha ha.*

But I returned. He asked his questions as he moved from table to table, wiping each one with a wet rag. I followed him as I answered. No, I had no experience. Yes, I was in high school. No, I hadn't taken any cooking courses. Yes, I could think ahead. He asked nothing about cleaning. Yet that was the job he offered me at the end of the interview. "One hour only. Every day. Six-fifty. You take?"

I nodded.

"You begin next month. First day."

Getting the job was easy enough, but convincing my father was another matter. Even after I explained that I would go to work only after spending an hour at the library. He asked so many questions. What kind of place would hire someone with no experience? How would

I work and study at the same time? What did I know of cleaning tables? How could he explain the job to all his relatives in all those other countries? He would have to say that his son was becoming a janitor.

In the end, it was Mom who convinced him. All she said was, "Aggy, this is not Uganda." Such a simple statement! I never realized Mom was so powerful.

I couldn't wait for the beginning of March. On the first day of the month, I went to Sip and Sup right after my library research. The owner was reading a newspaper. Without looking at me, he said, "Mop and pail stay on this side and apron on that side." He pointed to the left of the counter and then to the right. I waited for him to explain some more. After a minute or so, he lowered his newspaper and added, "You still here?"

"Shouldn't I clean the tables?"

"Clean table in dirty room like pretty woman with no upstairs. Hah!" He brought up his newspaper so it hid his face. His tiny cackle and shaking hands made me think he had made some sort of joke.

I put on the green apron and hauled the pail to one end of the place. It took me close to an hour to mop the floor and another twenty minutes to clean the tables. Throughout, I noticed the Chinese man peeking at me above his newspaper. Once, an old man with a red cap and a nose like a potato said to him, "See you got a new boy, Chum. Wonder how long this one's going to last?"

"We see, mister." He said this in a sad, tired way, as if he expected I would not return the next day. But I was determined. On my way home, I tried to imagine all the benefits of working in Sip and Sup. Once I got used to mopping, it would be far easier. And Mr. Chum might increase my hours and even offer me a job behind the counter. Mr. Chum himself looked a little grumpy, but he had a really friendly name. However, the best reward of all would be seeing my parents' face when I showed them my first pay.

Chapter Five

At the end of my first week at Sip and Sup, I realized that there were three groups of regular customers. They came every day and always chose the same tables. They also talked about the same topics. The old ladies sat just in front of the exit, dressed in what seemed like brand new coats and scarves. They usually talked about their dead husbands and about tulips. They were all powdered up, as if they had been invited to a tea party or something.

In the left corner sat a group of old men. I thought their wives must still be alive because unlike the old women they chatted mostly about wars and government stuff. Black men wearing puffy coats and baseball caps made up the third group. When they settled around their own table and began to talk and laugh loudly, the old men became quiet. They got lively only when the black men left to walk across the road to a high-rise building. The black men never stayed very long.

Before I started working, I had noticed the three or four young men who often sat at one of the outdoor tables. They watched the neighbourhood girls. Now I saw that they never came into Sip and Sup to order anything. I don't think Mr. Chum liked them hanging around the place. He would turn his newspaper pages roughly whenever he noticed them. Once I heard him grumbling about "idlers and roafers." I took a while to realize that he meant "loafers."

One day as I was leaving to go home, one of the loafers asked, "Hey, buddy, do you speak Chinese?"

When I said I didn't, the group began to laugh. The next day, another loafer called out, "Hey, buddy, where are you from?"

I guessed he meant before I moved to Ajax, so I answered, Napanee. Before that, another asked. New Brunswick, I told him.

"What a comedian," the first one said. He wasn't laughing, though.

When I got home, Mom asked her usual question: did I make any new friends? Mom felt that I was too shy and that I spent too much time in the library and on the computer. I blamed Allison for Mom's worries because she often called me "geek" and "nerd." Dad would take my side, though. "Talent without discipline is useless," he would say.

Anyway, that evening I told Mom that I had chatted for a minute with some boys outside the coffee shop. That seemed to put her in a really good mood. Then, during dinner, Dad told us about the new job he expected to begin soon.

"Is it in Toronto?" Allison asked.

"In Ajax, dear," Mom said. "Making cell phone batteries." I could tell my sister was disappointed and angry from the way she rapped her fork against her plate. I felt a little sorry for her, and I decided I would buy her a small gift when I got my first pay. Maybe a black wristband to match her necklace.

Chapter Six

I got my first pay exactly one month after I began working at Sip and Sup. Before Mr. Chum gave me the money, he waved it around as if it were a thousand dollars. "Now, don't go spending on trip to Hawaii. Hah."

As I made my way down the outside steps, one of the young men asked, "Hey, buddy, what are you holding in your pocket?"

"My first pay," I told him rather proudly.

A tall guy with a cap pulled low over his forehead had a slim beard running down his chin. It looked like a caterpillar. He said something about buying a detonator, which was strange. Why would I? I liked doing experiments and had sometimes thought of becoming a highway engineer, but there was no way he would know that.

I didn't go home directly but went into the dollar store that was next to the drugstore. I wanted to shop for gifts. When I was about to leave, I noticed that the cashier looked a little familiar. She had a scarf tied over her head. Maybe I had seen her at school. When I got home, almost an hour late, Mom was waiting by the door. She looked worried. Dad and Allison were already having dinner. "What's that?" Mom asked, looking at the two bags in my hands.

"I bought some gifts for you."

"Is it Christmas in April now?" Allison asked, but I didn't pay her any attention.

"I got my first pay today."

"And already you are wasting it on nonsense," Dad said.

"Be quiet, Aggy," Mom said, before Dad could begin one of his lectures about his brothers in Uganda saving every single penny. She turned to me. "What did you get us, dear?" I emptied the bags on the sofa.

Mom said, "Oh, how nice," and "This will come in handy," as she examined the vase and flowerpot and potato peeler and picture frame. She held up a light green lampshade. "This is perfect for your room, Allison. It will match the curtains." Whenever I bought her gifts, Mom always made me feel like I'd picked the perfect things.

I felt happy for the rest of the evening. Even when Mom warned me that I should always let her or Dad know when I planned to get home later than usual. I repeated what Allison had said months ago: Ajax is small and safe. All the crime and bad stuff happens elsewhere.

I really believed that. And when I got all A's in school, I imagined that this quiet town had played a small part. Mr. Chum even said he would give me an extra hour of work each day for the summer. I was as happy as I had been when I was a child in Fredericton.

Then one day I overheard the Sip and Sup old men talking about some big plot to blow up important buildings in Ottawa and Toronto. They were reading an article from the *Sun* newspaper. They appeared younger than usual, maybe because they were all worked up. Getting upset made their cheeks rosy. One of the men always wore a poppy pinned onto his coat. He kept his eyes on me the entire time I cleaned the table opposite the group.

When I left to go home, one of the loafers yelled at me, "Hey, comedian, what's your name?"

"Tommy."

"Yeah? What about your last name?"

I was about to say, Lohanna. Then I remembered how some of the boys at Prince Charles Public School in Napanee used to call me Lindsay, on account of my last name. As if I was Lindsay Lohan, that silly girl actress. I had felt so ashamed.

"Whatsa matter? Is it Mohammed?" I shook my head. As I walked away, I heard him shouting other names. "Ali? Hussein?"

When I got home, I learned more about what had bothered the old men so much. Mom and Dad sat in front of the television watching the news. The girl announcer had a worried smile. She was talking about the arrest of five or six young men earlier in the day. They belonged to some kind of group — the announcer called it a "terrorist cell."

The cell had been under secret observation by the police for a couple of months. A video clip showed the police leading the young men away in handcuffs. Then came an interview with a woman who insisted that they were all decent boys. They couldn't have been involved in this plot, she said. They all came from good families and got high grades at school. "They even like hockey," she added as the final proof of their innocence.

Mom felt sad. "Why would they want to blow up these places, anyway?" she said. "This is Canada, for goodness' sake. What have we ever done to anyone?"

She probably hoped mentioning Canada would keep Dad from throwing in some reference to Uganda. Surprisingly, it was Allison who responded.

"So what's new? Places get blown up every day. Check the news." She said this in her fake-bored voice, and when we all looked at her, she got up and added, "Remember the bombing in London that we saw on TV? Everyone's still talking about that, even though it happened more than a year ago. No one remembers the poor guy who got shot by the cops in the subway because he was the wrong colour. Brazilian or something."

I was about to ask how she knew this when she said, "Later. I have to study." She went into her room and closed the door.

"This girl," Mom said. "If it's not one new phase it's another." Maybe it was my imagination, but Mom didn't sound as playful as she usually did when commenting on one of Allison's new phases.

Chapter Seven

About two weeks into the new school term, I saw Allison in the cafeteria. She was sitting with the dollar store girl and another brown girl who looked a bit older. I wondered if Allison had broken up with the Goth girls, who were sitting at the far end of the cafeteria. Maybe she had made different friends in her new classes.

The dollar store girl smiled, and when Allison turned around and saw me, she frowned. As if I was spying on her. Still, I waved to the group. Dad would like Allison's new friends more than he liked the Goth girls.

Each week there was some newspaper story about the terrorist cell boys. The old men at Sip and Sup talked on and on about them. Surprisingly, so did the old ladies, who said things like, "You never know..." and "Could be anyone..." Their voices sounded the same as when they chatted about their dead husbands. Sort of sing-song and sad, as if they were playing with memories that were growing dimmer and dimmer each day.

One evening, I spotted the man with the caterpillar beard sitting by himself on a picnic table bench outside. Even though it was a chilly fall day, he wore just a sweatshirt with the sleeves rolled up. On his left wrist I noticed a tattoo of a little girl. I saw him watching me, so I asked, "Where are your friends today?"

"I don't keep tabs on them. Where are yours?"

"Friends? None to talk of."

"And why is that?" His voice matched the coldness in the air.

"Too busy with school and work." Because he seemed lonely sitting by himself, I added, "I'm working hard, because I'd like to become an engineer."

He looked away, towards a girl pushing a stroller through the parking lot. "Yeah, that's nice."

It seemed he wanted to be alone, so I walked off. A strong breeze was blowing the leaves off the sidewalk. I hoped the caterpillar man would go into the coffee shop. He had to be freezing.

The next day, I felt I had wasted my concern. Two of caterpillar man's friends were with him. "Hey, everyone. It's Terry," he said. His friends laughed. A short, ugly guy with spiky hair said, "What's up, Terry?"

"It's Tommy," I told them.

"No, I think it's Terry," the short guy replied.

"Suit yourself." As I walked up the steps, I heard them saying "Terry" over and over. As if it was a big joke. While I was cleaning the floor, I saw them glancing at me. I wondered what they were saying. I wished they knew more about me. Like how I was so sad when we moved from Fredericton. How I grew afraid of making new friends after that move. How much I hoped we would never move from Ajax. I pretended the caterpillar man was saying, "Kid wants to be an engineer. Good for him."

The old men had left early, but their cups and newspapers were still on their table. A copy of the *Star* newspaper lay open. I dusted off the crumbs and flipped through the pages. I froze when I got to page three.

There was a picture of one of the terrorist cell boys. He looked nervous and excited and proud. As if he was about to deliver a long speech in a room filled with strange people. But it was the paragraph under the photograph that caught my eye. It began, "First year engineering student caught in the web." Cell. Web. Terrorist. Explosion.

As I was about to fold the newspaper, I heard a loud clap. I jumped and turned. "Floor, get clean now! Mop, jump up and dance!" Mr. Chum clapped again. "Tables, get clean fast!" More clapping. "Oh, no, magic not work today. So sad. So sad."

I quickly got the pail and began mopping. What Mr. Chum had said was funny, but I could not smile. The guy in the newspaper seemed too familiar. Bright, an only son, kept to himself, was polite to his elders, and his parents had come from some other country. He was normal in every way except for his secret meetings.

All at once, I knew why the young men outside had insisted on calling me Terry. It was not a mistake for Tommy. They were calling me Terry because it was short for terrorist.

I should never have mentioned my interest in engineering. Earlier, I had wished they knew more about me. Now I was afraid they knew too much. At the end of my shift, I walked down the steps as fast as I could. I could still hear their mocking voices. *Terry. Terry. Terry.*

Chapter Eight

As I walked home, I remembered an unlucky boy from a long-ago story. This boy had a black cloud floating over his head. It followed him like a dirty, spiteful seagull. I looked up and saw a real black cloud. No, there were about a dozen. They looked like those animals that bit off parts of still-twitching prey. Hyenas or something. I walked faster, and by the time I got to our building, I was almost running.

"How was work today, dear?" Mom asked when I got home.

She asked that each evening, and as before, I told her, "Same as always."

"You look tired, though."

"I jogged home. It's good exercise."

"Why the change?" Allison didn't even bother looking up from the computer. I imagined her rolling her eyes and rocking her head. Just as she always did when Mom called me "chubby cheeks."

"It's better than changing into a new person every five minutes just to fit in."

"Whatever." The computer keys clicked. Maybe she was making fun of me with her Facebook friends.

During dinner, Mom and Dad talked about their usual stuff. I remained quiet, even when Mom said that she was happy I had stuck with my after-school job for so long.

I stayed at the table while everyone else went to watch television in the living room. But I could still see the TV. The announcer was interviewing some woman about the terrorist plot, a woman with curly red hair and an accent that made all her words seem zig-zagging. Even though she lived close to one of the accused boys, she said, she knew nothing of his family. "Quiet people, but who can tell anymore? Kept to themselves, you know…"

Mom said, "There's the cause, right there." Dad began talking about Uganda. At the end of the show, Allison hurried to her computer and began typing.

During my first week at Sip and Sup, I had worried that Mom or Dad would show up to check on me. Now I wished they would. Just to show the loafers outside that I had a normal family that didn't keep to themselves, a family that dressed like everyone else and spoke English better than most.

The next morning, as I was leaving for school, I said, "Hey, Mom, why don't you drop by the coffee shop today? There are nice muffins and donuts."

"Oh, that would be perfect for my diet." She gave me a little smile, but I jerked my head away before she could pinch my cheek.

All day at school, I tried to think of ways to deal with the loafers. Should I be friendly and force them to see that I was different from the cell boys? Or should I report them to Mr. Chum? I knew he did not approve of them hanging around outside his coffee shop. But what would I tell him? That they were calling me Terry? He would most likely laugh and make one of his jokes.

In the end, I decided I would ignore the loafers. So, as soon as I finished work, I put on my earphones, turned up the volume on my MP3 player, and hurried down the steps. But their voices cut through the music. Caterpillar man: "You wearing a listening device?" Short guy: "Yes, commander. I heard your orders. Over and out."

I began to hate this caterpillar man. First, because I had tried to be friendly with him once. And second, because he seemed to be the leader. So, when I noticed that the old men got quiet whenever I was cleaning the floor next to their table, I blamed him. I also blamed him when I spotted the old ladies gazing at me with their thin lips pressed into stiff smiles. And I blamed him when a complete stranger yelled something nasty to me from a pickup truck.

I had once liked this little town for its coziness, but now I began to dislike it for the same reason. I could see how easy it would be for rumours to spread. Everyone knew each other. I started to wish that Dad would announce we were leaving for a town far away from Ajax. Maybe if I ganged up with Allison we might be able to persuade our parents to leave.

When I got home, I saw Mom and Allison in the kitchen. Mom was arranging a head scarf on my sister's head. As soon as Allison went into her room, I asked Mom, "Why is Allison wearing a head scarf?"

Mom shrugged. "You know your sister. One new style after another."

"But why now? And why a head scarf? It's covering all her hair. Even her neck."

Allison started to yell something from her room. But from the living room, Dad shouted, "Why not? She looks nice in it. And it's not like she's joining a cult or anything."

But that was exactly what I thought. I was sure that the dollar store girl was responsible because she always wore a head scarf herself. I got angry with my sister for always being so easily influenced.

That night when my favourite television show, *The Big Bang Theory*, was on, I could not enjoy it. I kept thinking about how everyone was against me. Dad, for moving every few years. Mom, for still treating me like a child. Allison, for always trying to slip into a new identity. Even people who didn't know me were against me. The loafers, for connecting me with the terrorist cell boys. The cell boys, for pretending they were some kind of super-villains. Ajax itself had plotted against me by fooling me with its nice, quiet appearance. And I was to blame, too, for never, ever knowing how to fight back.

Chapter Nine

I had just one choice: I had to leave my job at Sip and Sup. Yet I knew that doing so would not solve the problem. Ajax was too small, and I could run into the loafers elsewhere. Besides, I had caught complete strangers staring at me.

I got angrier and angrier at the loafers. One day in the library, I got so mad that I couldn't work. I turned off the computer and looked through the window at the town hall.

Dad often said that, if only the army and the merchants in Uganda had been more patient with each other, his family wouldn't have had to leave. But what was the use of this patience? To the coffee shop crowd, I looked just like the terrorist cell boys, so I had to be one of them.

How dare they? What gave them a special right to this country? How would they feel if someone accused them of something so horrible?

I was still really mad that evening and I mopped the Sip and Sup floor as if I were the Flash. Mr. Chum said, "Super speed nice for superhero. Bad for mopping floor."

When I left, I did not wear my earphones. So I heard the caterpillar man clearly when he asked, "Done early, Terry? Going to meet your buddies?"

Words formed in my mind: *No, I prefer to loaf around and waste time.* But I knew that would sound just as childish and silly as one of my arguments with Allison. I didn't hurry away like I usually did, so I overheard the short guy trying to imitate some foreign language.

The short guy's noises reminded me of the language two brown boys at school used. One of the boys was in my English class. He was from Afghanistan, and he sat in the back row. Since September, he had been silent. Except for one time, when the teacher asked him a question. He didn't know the answer. While everyone was waiting for him, he had banged down his book on his desk, got up, and walked out of the classroom.

Like everyone else in the class, I had been annoyed with the boy from Afghanistan. Now I admired him. I was sure the loafers wouldn't pick on him, because he seemed ready for anything. Maybe his parents had taught him to fight instead of nonsense about politeness and self-control and good grades. Mom believed that the cure for everything was just fitting in. And I can't even count the times Dad had said, "If you can dream of it, you can get it." Yeah, sure. What was the use of being a dreamer when everyone else was awake?

This problem preyed on my mind. I thought of it during dinner, while Dad talked about his idol, the Aga Khan, who encouraged charity and all that. I thought of it during school, when I saw one of the boys from Afghanistan smoking behind the gym. And I thought of it each night on my way home from the coffee shop, with the words "Terry, Terry" ringing in my ears.

One evening, I saw the caterpillar man chatting with a woman who seemed about his age, twenty-four or so. I stood on the top step, pretending I was struggling to zip up my coat.

The woman was holding the hand of a little girl. She stood apart, as if she did not want to get too close to the caterpillar man. She pulled the child closer to her and said, "I've heard that before, Sid. Too many times." In a louder voice, she added, "Look at her. She doesn't recognize you anymore."

Just then, the caterpillar man — Sid — noticed me staring. "What the fuck are you looking at?"

The woman said, "See, this is what I'm talking about."

"You don't know anything." His voice sounded whiny.

The woman sighed. "I know that Lavinia doesn't recognize you anymore."

"And whose fault is that?"

"No one's, Sid. It's no one's fault." Her voice trailed off as she walked away in the opposite direction from me.

For once, this Sid man had nothing to say. I did not know why the young woman was so mad at him, but I was sure he deserved all of it.

Chapter Ten

For the next couple of weeks, I didn't see the loafers. Maybe they had chosen another coffee shop or been kicked out of Ajax. At the same time, Allison was behaving very strangely, always in front of the computer with her head scarf pulled tightly over her head.

Dad felt her new style was an improvement over her Goth look, but I could tell that it worried Mom. During our dinner-time conversations, Mom talked about the terrible things happening all over the world. Wars, kidnappings, and never-ending conflict. She blamed crazy traditions for each of these troubles.

Allison responded only once. She said that it was just as wrong to believe in one solution to fix every trouble. Mom was shocked, I could tell.

That night, I gazed at the water stain on the ceiling just above my bed. It looked like a boat about to sink. When I blinked and looked again, it changed into a rocket pointing upwards. I played this game for five minutes or so, trying to surprise myself with each new shape. But soon my mind turned to the dinner conversation. I wondered if Allison had taken on her new look because the girls at school had called her names. If the girls were doing to her what the loafers outside Sip and Sup were doing to me. Or if wearing a head scarf was a passing phase, just like the others. Whatever the reason, at least she had a group of friends.

The next morning on our way to school, Allison hurried to catch up with her friends. The dollar store girl waved to me. During recess, I noticed the Afghanistan boy standing outside the back door. He was gazing at the playing field. "Hey," I said.

"Hey." He barely glanced at me and kept staring into the distance. I guessed he wanted to be alone. Maybe the playing field reminded him of something from his country. I walked away. Even though we were the same colour, we were not alike. Our memories were too different. I had lived my entire life in Canada. His accent was Afghani.

In Napanee, there had been a Sikh boy in my class. He was the only other brown person in the school. Once he had shown me a tiny dagger tucked away in his pocket, and he explained why he carried it. When he asked me about my religion, all I could tell him was that my parents were Ismaili Muslims. The only fact I knew about my religion was that Sufis were important. They were poets who composed special religious songs.

He wanted to know more. I quoted a couple of my father's favourite Sufi verses, but that was the best I could do. Our friendship stalled at that point, maybe because he wished he hadn't shown me his dagger. Or maybe he felt there was something fake about a boy who knew so little of his parents' religion.

In the coffee shop, I felt really alone. The old ladies looked like pale ghosts that would soon disappear, the old men like forgotten statues.

Even Mr. Chum reading his newspaper looked to me like a cardboard cut-out set against the counter. At the end of my shift, he said, "Nice trick. Sleeping standing up. Hah!" He closed his eyes and pretended to snore. When he opened his eyes, he asked, "Whatsa matter, alligator?"

"It's nothing." I wondered if when I got home my family would also have been replaced with strangers.

Mr. Chum glanced at the outside table normally occupied by the loafers. He rolled up his newspaper slowly. "We control the picture," he said.

He returned to his newspaper, but I sensed his eyes on me while I put on my coat.

On my way home, I tried to understand what Mr. Chum meant. He often joked. Yet his voice had been serious. As I crossed the street at the corner of Harwood and Bayly, I realized that he had spoken with no trace of an accent. I had never heard this voice before. "We control the picture."

Chapter Eleven

"We control the picture." Mr. Chum's strange statement got my mind off my other worries. What did he mean? And why did he — just that once — speak without any accent? His simple sentence seemed familiar somehow, yet I could not tell why. I puzzled over it in school and in the coffee shop. I started to ask him once, but I changed my mind when I heard him once more speaking with his Chinese accent to some customer.

Then, one day in the library, I recalled the opening of a television series I used to watch with Dad in Napanee: *The Outer Limits*. As it opened, a man with a thin voice would say, "There is nothing wrong with your television set. Do not attempt to adjust the picture. We are controlling..." Each episode showed creatures that could change their shapes, or robots wanting to be humans, or aliens pretending to be ordinary families.

While I mopped and cleaned the coffee shop, I would glance at Mr. Chum, thinking about his remark. A couple of times, he caught me looking at him, and he returned to his newspaper without smiling or anything.

Yet Mr. Chum had become a more interesting person. Just from that simple statement. It reminded me of one of Dad's mysterious quotes from Shakespeare: *This is the tune of our catch, played by the picture of Nobody*. I imagined a boy walking through a house with a hundred doors inside it. Each time he passed through a door, he was different in some way. He was a nobody because he could be whatever he wanted to be. The picture of nobody was the picture of someone who could change into anyone.

I almost forgot all my worries, but then, a few weeks later, I was brought back to earth. The woman I had seen Sid chatting with started coming to the Sip and Sup regularly. She would arrive with her child by midway through my shift. The other loafers always left as soon as she appeared, and Sid and the woman would talk seriously.

Sometimes the woman appeared to be pleading. Once when Sid tried to play with her little girl, she pulled the child away. She usually left about ten minutes before the end of my shift. Sid would remain there at the table, his head in his hands. He seemed to be talking to himself, and a few times, he got up and waved his arms, even though no one was with him.

Sid also acted meaner to me. Before, his nasty remarks seemed like jokes to amuse his friends, but now he seemed serious — and dangerous, even. He said things like, "Where the hell do you people keep appearing from?" and "I have my eyes on you. Just remember that. This ain't Kabul."

One evening, the argument between Sid and the woman seemed to be worse than usual. She didn't sit for the entire half hour, and she held her girl tightly.

When she left in a huff, Sid clasped his hands at the back of his neck and bent low over the table. He seemed smaller, somehow, through the glass wall of the coffee shop. When I left, he was still in that same position. He said in a low voice, as if he was talking to himself, "Fucking Arab." He made the word sound like "crab."

I stopped in my tracks. "I'm not an Arab. I was born in Canada." After a while, I added, "Just like you."

"You're nothing like me, buddy."

"Yes, I know."

He glared at me as if he couldn't tell whether I had agreed with his statement or insulted him.

When I got home, Mom and Dad were in the dining room wearing their going-out clothes. "We are taking Allison to the Driftwood Theatre," Mom said. "To see *King Lear*. Sure you don't want to come along?"

I shook my head. "Too tired."

"*The weight of this sad time we must obey*," Dad said. "*Speak what we feel, not what we ought to say*."

Allison came out of her room as Dad was reciting the lines from the play. She rolled her eyes and, just for a moment, she looked like her old self.

"We will be back in two hours," Mom told me. "Keep the door locked."

As I dropped my backpack on the living room couch, I noticed the computer monitor glowing in the corner. I stared at Allison's Barbie screen saver. At another time, I may have felt touched that this screen saver had remained her favourite through all of her different phases. Valley Girl. Skater Girl. Goth. Head-scarf Girl. But I was in a different mood. When I sat at the computer desk, I noticed that she had left her Facebook and e-mail accounts open.

What I did next was something I never would have done if I had thought it through. It was one of those acts a person commits because the chance will vanish swiftly. It reminded me of the thin, feathery thrill I felt during our hidden treasure hunts in primary school.

And I felt this thrill as I created a new e-mail account; as I pasted all of Allison's contacts — there must have been more than fifty — into a viral e-mail; as I wrote that unbelievably nasty thing about "Sid who hangs out at Sip and Sup." But just as quickly, the excitement began to fade. I pressed Send before I could change my mind, and then I deleted the new e-mail account.

Chapter Twelve

The next morning I tried to convince myself that those who received the e-mail would ignore it as childish and silly. In any case, nothing could be traced back to me because I had deleted the account.

Such was my mental state that I pretended I would never, ever write such a horrible e-mail. Surely, sending this message was just my fantasy of revenge. I tried to chase away the thought that what I had written might even be true.

Yet that evening I got a clue that I had really done something big. Even though the loafers came to their usual spot, Sid did not turn up. Midway through my shift, the woman with the little girl came, and she talked to the group for a while. Although she remained there for close to fifteen minutes, none of the loafers ever looked up at her. I think they were glad when she left. They moved closer to each other and seemed to be whispering.

I didn't see the loafers again until Friday. That day, a police car pulled up, and a pretty female officer walked over to them. The officer did most of the talking. Even though she got into her car after just three or four minutes, the conversation had seemed never-ending to me.

All sorts of questions ran through my mind. What was she asking them? What did they tell her? But the question that stuck throughout that night was: could the e-mail be traced back to me? Deep down, I knew the officer's visit was connected to what I had written about Sid.

I tossed and turned almost all that night. Each time the single sentence tried to wriggle into my head, I made myself think of something else. I tried to think of how happy I had been in Fredericton. The students at my school there thought my brown face meant that I was Native. I wished I could still pretend to be someone else. Anyone who could not be connected with bombs and secret plots. But, I thought, it's too late now. I had dug a deep hole and jumped straight into it.

I suffered day and night, but soon this worry was replaced by another. Although the loafers did not show up the next week, the woman with the girl did. She stayed by the usual table even after my shift was over, holding her child and staring into the distance.

One evening there was a snowstorm. The snow brightened up the street so much that I could clearly see everyone hurrying to their homes. I could see the cars driving by slowly. And I could see the woman sitting with her child as if she was stuck there and needed someone to pull her away. The little girl tried to do that once. She couldn't make her mother move, so she sat at the end of the bench with her small arms folded against her chest. The large, twirling snowflakes looked to me like bleached cockroaches crowding the child. This scene felt like my punishment, yet I couldn't look away. I got annoyed with myself because I was so warm and comfortable in the coffee shop.

I walked over to Mr. Chum and told him, "The little girl outside seems to be freezing."

He looked up from his newspaper. "You ask her to come inside."

I couldn't tell from his flat voice whether he was asking a question or not. Still, I leaned the mop against the counter and walked down the steps. "Do you want to come inside? It's really cold out here."

The woman did not answer, but the girl looked up at me. Her cheeks were completely red. "Mama?" She tugged at her mother's coat.

I stood there for a minute or so, waiting for the mother to say something, and when she did not, I returned to the coffee shop. I began to wipe the tables, but I kept my head down so I wouldn't see the mother and her child freezing outside.

Shortly before the end of my shift, I heard Mr. Chum say, "Rittle baby fleezing. Hey, Tommy. Chocoritt for baby." He held up a cup.

I took the hot chocolate to the little girl. When I saw her mother holding back, I told her, "Don't bother paying. Mr. Chum told me to give it to her." She opened the cup's cover as her daughter eased onto her lap.

At the end of my shift, as I was leaving, the woman asked me, "What's your name?"

"Tommy."

"Thanks, Tommy."

I should have been relieved, but those two words made me feel worse than ever. She had nothing to thank me for.

Chapter Thirteen

Each evening, from then on, the young woman came into Sip and Sup with her child. She sat at a corner table, not smiling or talking with anyone, just staring outside. It seemed she was scanning the parking lot, searching for Sid. Once, one of the old ladies walked over and asked her, "How old is the pretty girl?"

"Three."

"What's her name?" She smiled in her frozen manner at the child.

"Lavinia."

"Lavinia? That's an unusual name."

"Yeah."

After that, the old ladies left her alone, but sometimes I caught them glancing at her and whispering to each other.

During one of these conversations, I went to a nearby table with my rag. One thin old lady had flowery patterns on her sweater and a thick blue vein on the side of her neck. She was talking in a soft voice. I moved closer and heard the lady say, "She's made some bad choices. It's always the little ones who suffer. The innocent ones." The entire group went silent, as if they were thinking deeply about these little ones.

The following day, another woman said, "Her father's a preacher, too, wouldn't you know. I wonder what the poor man thinks of this whole mess." I waited for some explanation, but once again, the group got quiet. I wished I could read the minds of these old women who preferred silence to normal talk. Maybe they were thinking that life was simpler when they were young.

Throughout all of the talk around her, the woman with the child just stared outside, as if she was the only person in the place. Whenever she spotted young men leaving the bus terminal, she would become alert and pull Lavinia closer. Sometimes the black men in the puffy jackets would glance at her while they were waiting for their coffees. I wondered if they, too, wished she would smile instead of looking so unhappy. She never did, even when Mr. Chum came over and greeted the child in a silly baby voice.

It was Mr. Chum who told me one evening, "Father just disappear. So sad. So sad."

"The father of the little girl? Where did he go?"

He shrugged. "Back to Oshawa. Good for pretty lady. Now she can start over. Get job somewhere. Maybe I fire you and hire her. Hah. She here every day in any case. Now give baby this muffin."

Later, my mother asked me, "Is everything okay at work, Tommy?"

"Yes, yes," I answered quickly. I noticed Allison looking at me from the computer desk.

Mom was always good at detecting my problems. She felt my sadness after we left Fredericton. She knew how ashamed I was when the boys in Napanee called me Lindsay Lohan —

not just a foolish person, but a girl, too. And when Allison teased me and called me a geek because I had no friends.

Thankfully, Dad walked through the door just then. He was holding a pizza. "*Win her with gifts, if she respect not words,*" he said, bowing and placing the pizza before Mom. Usually Allison would roll her eyes at Dad's corny quotations and romantic acts. Once again, though, I noticed her looking at me in a strange manner. She did the same during dinner.

By the time we finished eating, I was certain Allison knew what I had done. Perhaps I had left some trail in the computer. Or maybe she found it strange that all her friends had received the same brief message. They would certainly gossip about such a thing on Facebook.

After Allison and Dad left the table, Mom asked, "Can you help me with the dishes, Tommy?" She turned on the tap, and the spurting water covered the sound of her voice. She said, "You have been very quiet lately, Tommy. More than usual. You hardly say a word to anyone."

Dad appeared carrying a dish towel. "Words must touch us here." He pointed to his chest.

"They must have melody. They must float and dance and sing and…"

"Words must have rules," Mom said, without looking up from the sink. "They must show us how to act." I felt she was soothing me and warning me at the same time. But all I could think of was how dangerous words were.

Chapter Fourteen

For three weeks, I imagined the worst. Maybe Sid was in a prison somewhere, being tortured for information he could not give. Or he was on the run, moving from town to town, always watching over his shoulder. I imagined Lavinia, years from now, still asking her mother if he would ever return. I pictured both mother and child forever waiting, forever staring at the GO bus terminal, forever unhappy.

The spiteful act that led to this situation had been done quickly, before I had time to think about its effects. I decided to be more cautious in making my next decision. I watched the old ladies whispering to themselves. I studied the expressions of the old men as they slowly walked past the little girl. I saw how all their attention had shifted from me to the pair. I listened to Mr. Chum joke each evening about firing me to hire the woman. One evening he said, "I think baby like this place. Maybe is nice cake smell."

I told him of my decision quickly, before I could change my mind. "Mr. Chum, I will have to leave next week. The end of the month."

"Leave? Why you leave? After all the free training?" His loud voice awoke the little girl. She gazed sleepily at the chocolate in Mr. Chum's hand and reached for it.

In my mind, I went over all the excuses I had prepared. The constant mopping and sweeping was too difficult. The work was affecting my studies. It was really my parents' decision. Yet, when I saw the woman watching me with her big sad eyes, all of the lies stuck in my throat. It seemed as if she was trying to read my mind.

Mr. Chum saved me from lying. "Okay," he said. "I hire mother. Baby stay as decoration."

"Me? I've never worked in a coffee shop before."

"Oh, so easy. So easy. If Tommy does it then anybody can. Hah!"

My father, for one, seemed relieved when I told him that I'd quit. He'd be glad that he would never have to explain to his foreign relatives that his son was mopping and sweeping a coffee shop. Mom didn't say anything, which was unusual. However, later, while I was helping her with the dishes, she asked, "Are you going to look for another job?"

"Not right now."

She was rinsing the cups longer than usual, as if she had something on her mind. For just a second, I wanted to tell her everything. I would explain how I had taken revenge on Sid by spreading this rumour about him. I would confess that I never knew it would affect other people. Especially not a sad woman and her little girl. I would say that I never suspected that rumours could be so hurtful to innocent people. They were like fires that could never be put out. I had learned my lesson well.

But that brief moment passed when I noticed Allison by the fridge. She was looking straight at me.

Chapter Fifteen

Mr. Chum soon grew quite attached to Lavinia. Sometimes, on my way home from the library, I would see him standing in front of her with a treat in his hand. I imagined him cooing to her constantly while her mother was cleaning the place. About a month after I left the job, I spotted the mother behind the counter for the first time. I guess she had been promoted.

Dad smiled when I showed him my latest grades. "Good job," he said. Mom said something similar. And, for the first time, Allison did not look offended by these compliments.

Why had Allison's attitude towards me changed? Had she figured out what I had done? Did her discovery change me from a chubby, pesky brother into someone mysterious? Did my unhappiness keep her from giving away my secret?

Maybe she had just grown up a bit, and I hadn't noticed. Anyway, she no longer seemed in a hurry to leave Ajax. Perhaps she had found in this little town what she had hoped to find in Toronto.

One night during dinner, Mom told us a story I had never heard before. A woman who had recently come to Canada had prepared herself for her new country in every single way she could think of. She stepped off the plane carrying a briefcase filled with newspaper clippings about Canada.

I thought Mom was on this lady's side, but no. The woman soon began to see herself in these clippings. *She* was the woman who would never be hired to a top job. *She* was the woman who would always live in some crowded part of Toronto. The woman who would be mocked for her accent and pitied for her shyness.

I remembered my story of the house with one hundred doors and the boy who walked through them all. But this woman had gotten stuck at the first door. She could not even see all the other doors.

Dad chimed in with one of his favourite Sufi sayings: *When the heart weeps for what it has lost, the spirit rejoices for what it has gained.* Corny, as usual, but I pretended he was telling me that hidden inside every bit of sadness is some important lesson. Maybe Mom was telling me that I could be anyone I chose. I was not a terrorist or a geek or a terrorist geek because other people said so. I didn't have to remain stuck at the first door.

I could be anyone I chose. The choice was mine. Perhaps Allison had been one step ahead of me all the time. She had been able to control her picture. I glanced at her and felt I was seeing her in a new way. Not as a whiny pest, but as a kind of adventurer.

I pretended that Allison and I were having a conversation about Ajax. I imagined telling her that I was wrong to blame the town for my recent problems. It was just bad luck that I had met Sid and the other loafers. But I had also met Mr. Chum and the sad mother and her pretty little girl.

That was my good luck. In our imaginary conversation, I told Allison that just this morning, as I was passing Sip and Sup, the woman saw me through the glass door. She whispered something to Lavinia. The child stood up on a chair and waved to me. The woman seemed happier than I had ever seen her.

Maybe she, too, had chosen to be someone new.

Good ⬛Reads

Discover Canada's Bestselling Authors with Good Reads Books

Good Reads authors have a special talent—
the ability to tell a great story, using clear language.

Good Reads books are ideal for people

✳ on the go, who want a short read;
✳ who want to experience the joy of reading;
✳ who want to get into the reading habit.

To find out more, please visit
www.GoodReadsBooks.com

The Good Reads project is sponsored by
ABC Life Literacy Canada.

The project is funded in part by the Government of Canada's
Office of Literacy and Essential Skills.

Libraries and literacy and education markets
order from Grass Roots Press.

Bookstores and other retail outlets order from HarperCollins Canada.

Good Reads Series

If you enjoyed this Good Reads book,
you can find more at your local library or bookstore.

2010

The Stalker by Gail Anderson-Dargatz
In From the Cold by Deborah Ellis
Shipwreck by Maureen Jennings
The Picture of Nobody by Rabindranath Maharaj
The Hangman by Louise Penny
Easy Money by Gail Vaz-Oxlade

2011 Authors

Joseph Boyden
Marina Endicott
Joy Fielding
Robert Hough
Anthony Hyde
Frances Itani

For more information on Good Reads,
visit **www.GoodReadsBooks.com**

Easy Money
by Gail Vaz-Oxlade

Wish you could find a money book that doesn't make your eyes glaze over or your brain hurt? Easy Money is for you.

Gail knows you work hard for your money, so in her usual honest and practical style she will show you how to make your money work for you. Budgeting, saving, and getting your debt paid off have never been so easy to understand or to do. Follow Gail's plan and take control of your money.

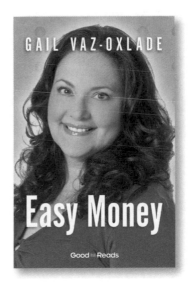

Shipwreck
by Maureen Jennings

A retired police detective tells a story from his family's history. This is his story...

On a cold winter morning in 1873, a crowd gathers on the shore of a Nova Scotia fishing village. A stormy sea has thrown a ship onto the rocks. The villagers work bravely to save the ship's crew. But many die.

When young Will Murdoch and the local priest examine the bodies, they discover gold and diamonds. They suspect that the shipwreck was not responsible for all of the deaths. With the priest's help, Will—who grows up to be a famous detective—solves his first mystery.

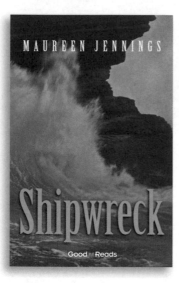

The Hangman
by Louise Penny

On a cold November morning, a jogger runs through the woods in the peaceful Quebec village of Three Pines. On his run, he finds a dead man hanging from a tree.

The dead man was a guest at the local Inn and Spa. He might have been looking for peace and quiet, but something else found him. Something horrible.

Did the man take his own life? Or was he murdered? Chief Inspector Armand Gamache is called to the crime scene. As Gamache follows the trail of clues, he opens a door into the past. And he learns the true reason why the man came to Three Pines.

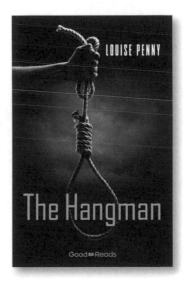

The Stalker
by Gail Anderson-Dargatz

Very early one Saturday morning, Mike's phone rings. "Nice day for a little kayak trip, eh?" says the deep, echoing voice. "But I wouldn't go out if I were you."

Mike's business is guiding visitors on kayak tours around the islands off the west coast. This weekend, he'll be taking Liz, his new cook, and two strangers on a kayak tour. Soon, his phone rings again. "I'm watching you," the caller says. "Stay home."

Mike and the others set off on their trip, but the

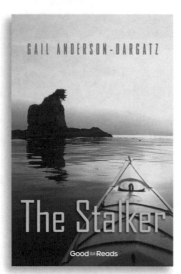

stalker secretly follows them. Who is he? What will he do? *The Stalker* will keep you guessing until the end.

In From the Cold

by Deborah Ellis

Rose and her daughter Hazel are on the run in a big city. During the day, Rose and Hazel live in a shack hidden in the bushes. At night, they look for food in garbage bins.

In the summer, living in the shack was like an adventure for Hazel. But now, winter is coming and the nights are cold.

Hazel is starting to miss her friends and her school. Rose is trying to do the right thing for her daughter, but everything is going so wrong. Will Hazel stay loyal to her mother, or will she try to return to her old life?

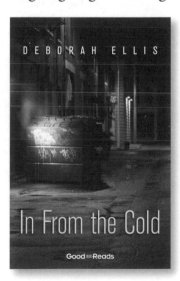

About the Author

 Through his writing, Rabindranath Maharaj helps readers to understand the immigrant experience. *Homer in Flight* was a finalist for the Chapters/*Books in Canada* First Novel Award and *A Perfect Pledge* was a *Globe and Mail* Best Book. Robin was born and raised in Trinidad. He immigrated to Canada in the early 1990s and lives in Ajax, Ontario.

Also by Rabindranath Maharaj:

The Interloper
The Writer and His Wife
Homer in Flight
The Lagahoo's Apprentice
The Book of Ifs and Buts
A Perfect Pledge
The Amazing Absorbing Boy

You can visit Rabindranath's website at
rmaharaj.wordpress.com